OLIVER
Saves the Nature Center

Andrew Kranichfeld
illustrated by Sally Tobin

Dedication

This book is dedicated to my older brother Oliver. His intelligence, kindness, curiosity, warm spirit, and zest for life will always inspire me.

Special thanks to:

Henry Kranichfeld III for everything

Libby Kingsbury and Margaret Turton for help with formatting, layout, and publishing

Neil Mendick for editorial help

Sally Tobin for her beautiful illustrations

Sara Bannet and the students of John Hanson Montessori School

Kendall Ramsey and the students of Suitland Elementary

Heather and Petra Smith

The Bruce Museum

The Rye Nature Center

The Marshlands Conservancy

The Edith G. Read Wildlife Sanctuary

Ella Pastor

Lamoussa Felicite Kologo

Melanie Wachtell-Stinnett

Dave Regan of armoredpenguin.com for crossword and word search puzzles

"The only way forward, if we are going to improve
the quality of the environment, is to get everyone involved."

—Richard Rogers.

1

The Problem

Oliver walked down the wooded path. He was headed to the pond to do some work on the overgrown vegetation. When he arrived at the pond, he began clipping back some bushy shrubs and pulling weeds from the ground.

Oliver was an environmental educator at the nature center. When he wasn't teaching students about nature and the environment, he helped maintain the grounds. As he knelt down to gather some fallen leaves, he heard a voice over his shoulder.

"Are you the one who was sent to help us?" asked the old, scratchy voice.

Oliver slowly turned his head and looked around.

"Ahhhhh," he yelled in disbelief. All he saw was a large, black-and-red painted turtle, staring him right in the eyes. He held his garden shears up in self-defense. "Who said that?!" he screamed, turning his head from side to side.

"Why, it was me, of course," answered the turtle. "I am just asking if you are the one who was sent to help us animals."

"No, I just work here at the nature center. I teach the students about nature, ecology, and the environment."

"Well, if you don't help us soon, there won't be much of an environment left to teach about. It is rapidly declining and needs your help immediately!" replied the turtle. "Come with me, and I will show you the problems that we local animals and our plant friends are facing."

Am I dreaming? Oliver thought. He pinched his arm. "Ouch!" he quietly whispered as he turned and followed the old turtle down the trail. Oliver and the mysterious turtle arrived at a bridge just outside the woods. Across the bridge was the town, where there were bustling businesses, big buildings, and a plethora of people.

"What is your name?" Oliver asked the turtle.

"There are some who know me as Oscar, the wise one, but my real name is Rolando Flapperjacks."

"Rolando Flapperjacks?!" Oliver laughed. "That is the most ridiculous name I have ever heard!"

"Well, your name, Oliver, sounds just as ridiculous to us animals! But let's focus on the urgent matter at hand—my dwindling habitat!" said the turtle sternly. "As you can see here, some people from town are using this area as their dumping grounds. Not only is the garbage killing local fauna like frogs, fish, and even turtles, but the chemical runoff is also contaminating the brook. This is causing some of the local flora to die." Oscar continued as he walked along the water's edge, with Oliver listening attentively. "And the sad part is, most of this trash can be recycled."

Oliver inspected the waste scattered along the stream. There were some empty aluminum cans, glass bottles, cardboard cartons, and plastic shopping bags. Along with the garbage, there was organic waste including food, fallen leaves, and grass clippings. Oliver frowned with sadness and concern. He was unaware there was so much garbage and waste so close to the nature center.

As the two moved along the waterway, they came upon a flooded section of the brook. There was water damage to some of the nearby houses and stores, but even worse, there were many dead fish floating on the surface of the water.

Oliver analyzed the situation and then asked, "Is this created by the runoff problem?"

"Yes," Oscar answered. "You and the other humans have overdeveloped this area. There are too many buildings, roads, and parking lots and not enough grass and soil. So the storm water is no longer being properly absorbed. This is causing the flooding problems in the area. Pollutants such as fertilizers, pesticides, and bacteria contaminate the same water that we both need to survive. The pollutants can come from many places, but a majority of this seems like agricultural pollution. It is washed from farms into our local waterways: the Hudson River, Long Island Sound, the duck pond, and eventually to the Atlantic Ocean. That is what killed all of those innocent, friendly fish who were just minding their own business."

Oliver thought hard, holding his thumb and forefinger to his chin. "I am not sure how to deal with the construction problem. Many people today would rather have another shopping mall or an extra bedroom instead of a nice green park or bigger yard. But I could distribute rain barrels to local residents and businesses. They will greatly reduce the amount of runoff and flooding in the area. They also save water that can be used for tasks in times of drought."

"Well, thank heavens you humans can do something useful! Follow me, and I will show you the other environmental emergencies," said the wise, old turtle.

"Can you move a little faster?" asked Oliver.

"Haven't you ever heard of 'slow and steady'?" retorted Oscar. "That's how you win the race. And I am almost one hundred and fifty years old. Let's see how you're doing at one hundred and fifty!"

"I apologize. I had no idea you were so old. You look great for one hundred and fifty," Oliver said in awe as they descended the hill and arrived at an estuary. On one side of the peninsula, tiny saltwater waves rolled up onto the beach. On the other side, freshwater flowed from the brook and mixed with the water of the sound. This created beautiful salt marshes that were teeming with many different types of plants. There were also large sand dunes, which helped protect the fragile ecosystem.

As Oliver and Oscar reached the far side of the dunes, they saw several cars parked on top of the sand.

Did you know?

- One inch of rain on a thousand-square-foot roof will generate about six hundred gallons of runoff.

- Sand dunes can provide habitats for many different types of animals. Some examples include insects, crabs, mollusks, and shore birds.

"You see, Oliver? These inconsiderate humans park right on the dunes! They don't even think about the harm they are doing to our local environment! These sand dunes help in many ways. They act as a reservoir of sand to replenish the beach in times of erosion. The plants growing in them can stabilize and help protect the coastline. Also the exhaust from these cars contains harmful compounds like carbon monoxide, which poisons the air that we have to breathe. This is harmful to local animals such as blue jays, squirrels, humans, and of course, turtles!"

"I have a simple fix for this problem. We can just rope off the dunes so that cars can no longer park on them, but I don't know if I'd consider this an emergency!" said Oliver.

"Well, humans often underestimate the damage they are doing to Mother Nature. These dunes and the estuary are vital parts of this ecosystem. Estuaries are considered the nurseries of the sea. Thousands of different species of birds, fish, and other animals come to these protected waters to reproduce and feed."

"You're right; I'm sorry. Is there anything else to add to the list?"

"There is something else, but it is back at the nature center," the turtle mumbled as he plodded back down the road. They finally arrived at a dilapidated greenhouse. Many of the windows were broken into jagged shards of glass, and the planting beds were missing soil. There were broken clay pots, flickering light bulbs on the ceiling, and a beat-up hose with many creases and holes in it.

"You want me to fix this place up?" Oliver wondered. "But how is that going to help the environment?"

"Because everything is connected, Oliver," answered Oscar. "If you grow fruits and vegetables here, they can help feed your community. This way, less food will have to be shipped from far away by trucks and planes. And with fewer vehicles shipping food from afar, there will be less pollution.

"Also, if you grow the food yourself, you can eat it straight from the vine. It won't have to be packaged in materials like plastic and styrofoam, which could eventually end up back in the brook or other waterways. And when foods come from far away, they are often sprayed with harmful preservatives that have to be washed off before eating them."

"I must thank you, Oscar. I knew humans were negatively affecting your animal friends and the environment, but I had no idea how dire the situation was. I am going to help! I want to make sure that the next generation of humans and all other living things has a clean, safe, and healthy environment to enjoy. They deserve a beautiful environment where they can live, grow, and raise their own families." The turtle stared blankly back at Oliver.

"Right, Oscar?" asked Oliver. The turtle tilted his head to the side and continued to stare for a second. Oliver scratched his head with a confused look. The turtle blinked a few times, turned around, and wandered off into the woods.

"Well, off to work!" Oliver said with a determined look in his eyes.

Did you know?

While organic waste can be broken down in as little as six weeks, Styrofoam takes more than one million years to decompose.

Did you know?

The first Earth Day was celebrated in the United States on April 22, 1970. Starting in 1990, the entire world began to partake in this important event.

2

Earth Day

Oliver placed flyers around town requesting help from local volunteers and asked on the sign-up sheet that they meet up at the nature center on April 22, which is Earth Day. When he arrived at the center on that day, he was pleasantly surprised at the turnout—a crowd of about fifteen people waiting for him. They were all community members, and most were friends of his younger brother, Andrew. He saw Scotty, Rayana, Alvaro, Adam, Jeff, and Eddie.

Rayana had moved to town from Vermont and liked snowboarding and listening to music. Alvaro had moved from Spain, where he loved watching soccer and enjoying the outdoors. Both Eddie and Adam played football together in junior league and were volunteer camp counselors at the local recreation center. Scotty was Andrew's best friend. They played street hockey, biked, went to the movies, and did just about everything together. Of all of Andrew's friends, Jeff enjoyed nature and the outdoors most of all. He liked to camp, fish, snowboard, surf, hike through mountains, and play baseball.

Andrew emerged from the group. "Hi, Oliver. I asked my sixth-grade friends to volunteer, and they all agreed. So we should have enough people to get everything done." While Oliver was saying hello to everyone, he felt a tugging on his shoe. He slowly looked down and saw an unforgettable face: Lila's flat piggy-nose, floppy ears, and buggy eyes stared at him with his shoelaces in her mouth.

"Lila?" he exclaimed. "What in the world are you doing all the way down here in New York?"

"I was going up to Maine for a fire hydrant sniffing tour and to visit Aunt Jodie. But I guess I took a wrong turn on Interstate 95. Since I was in the area, I thought I would stop by and lend a paw."

"So you can talk now, too?" asked Oliver to the piggy-tailed pug.

"I could always talk. I just find many of your human conversations to be completely mindless and boring. Most of the things you talk about involve reality television, celebrity gossip, or sports."

Oliver turned to the group. "Well, everyone, we couldn't have asked for a more beautiful day. We have a considerable amount of work ahead of us, but I think we can get it all done if we start right away. Our first project is to clean up the brook. Someone has been using it as his dumping grounds!"

Oliver led them down to the water, and he and the crew began picking up the trash. They gathered and sorted all of the different kinds of recycling, putting each piece in the correct bin.

"There are different bins for cardboard, plastic, aluminum, and glass," Oliver explained as they worked. "For those who haven't learned yet, recycling is a process where we can transform these old, damaged materials

into new, usable ones. This amazing process helps to keep waste from polluting our environment. It also keeps us from exhausting some of our most important raw materials." Oliver then pointed at some bins standing by the side of the brook. "And these special green bins are for composting. If you find organic waste such as leaves, grass clippings, or food, put it in the green containers."

"What is composting?" asked Andrew as he wiped the sweat from his brow.

"Composting is nature's way of recycling organic and biodegradable materials," answered Oliver. "It can take these grass clippings, those fallen leaves, and these decaying banana peels and process them into rich, healthy soil for the garden. It also benefits the environment in several ways. Some examples are that it makes the soil retain water and carry more nutrients for the plants that will grow in it, and it will help control pest problems."

"It will also save money," added Eddie. "Now we won't have to buy fertilizers or harmful pesticides for the greenhouse."

"And it will get these pesky fleas off my neck, right?" asked Lila, scratching her neck vigorously.

"No, Lila, not those kinds of pests. I mean insects like aphids, Japanese beetles, and cutworms, which will harm and even kill some of the plants we'll grow. So make sure you save organic waste in the green bins!"

Oliver and his crew worked very hard for a few hours until the entire brook was clean.

"Now," Oliver asked, "does anyone know any ways to prevent pollution in the first place?"

"I learned about reduce, reuse, and recycle in school," replied Rayana.

"Exactly, Rayana. Those are all essential ways to help the environment. To reduce your waste, try using products that have less packaging. One way to do this is to buy products in bulk and then make individual portions yourself. Fresh fruits and vegetables that come with little or no packaging are even better. Can you guys think of some examples of foods that are overpackaged?"

"Those small cereal boxes," said Adam. "I just take Cheerios from a large box and portion them into small reusable bags. That way I have my Cheerios everywhere I go!"

"Cheese!" exclaimed Alvaro. "Instead of those individually wrapped slices, I get a big block of manchego and cut off my own pieces."

Did you know?

- When you recycle an aluminum can, it can be turned into a new can within six weeks. If you throw it in the trash, it can take up to one million years to decompose.

- The average American uses about 160 gallons of water every single day!

- Pesticides are the only toxic substance humans release into the environment to intentionally kill other living things.

"Raisins and prunes seem to be overpackaged," Jeff pointed out. "Do they have to put each individual prune in its own wrapper? I just buy them from the health food store and keep them in glass jars."

"Those are all great ideas! And they are all essential to reducing the amount of waste we are creating," Oliver stated.

"And I can buy a giant bag of dry dog food instead of buying expensive, individually packaged lamb tenderloins," snorted out Lila.

"Uhhh, yeah…sure, Lila," Oliver said as he sarcastically mocked the piggy-tailed pug. "We should give out some recycling and composting bins out to local businesses to make sure they aren't creating any unnecessary waste. We have covered reducing and recycling pretty well. Does anyone know about reusing?"

"At my home, we don't use paper towels," announced Scotty. "We just use cloth rags that we can wash and use over and over again."

"Same here," Rayana said. "We also reuse airtight glass containers where my mom puts my favorite snack: maple walnut granola. We use the same ones for leftovers and for storing dried fruits and nuts."

"I know in my family we always shop with reusable cloth bags. This helps keep all of those plastic bags from polluting our town," added Eddie.

"Great," Oliver exclaimed. "It seems like you all have a pretty strong grasp of the concept of reduce, reuse, and recycle. You can make a big difference if you make these practices part of your daily routine. One thing that we haven't mentioned yet is to never use disposable products that you use only once and then throw away. Some examples are Styrofoam cups and plastic cutlery. They go against all three of our important principles of reduce, reuse, and recycle."

"Would reducing the number of cats help the environment in any way?" Lila prodded Oliver. "Because I am really quite sick of all cats!"

Oliver ignored Lila's off-topic question, and the group walked up the path.

"Now I wanted to talk a little about the runoff problem," Oliver said as they came upon the corner of a large building. "Wait here and I will be back in a minute."

Scotty was playing fetch with Lila, but after one of his throws, she disappeared into the thick brush. Right then, Oliver came around the corner, rolling a very large plastic barrel.

"Do you know what this is for?" asked Oliver as he positioned the barrel underneath the rain gutter of the building.

"To bathe small smelly doggies?!" Lila asked awkwardly as the stick fell from her mouth.

"No," answered Oliver. "This is a rain barrel. Rain barrels reduce runoff by capturing the rain from buildings and other structures. They are also useful because they help conserve water. For example, the same water, saved after a storm, can later be used to nourish the plants in your garden."

"And it is always good to have an emergency water supply," Andrew pointed out. "You can never have too much extra water around."

"Exactly. So we will need to distribute some rain barrels to local residents and businesses. But for now we better get going on our next project. It is down by the estuary and the sand dunes."

After a short hike, the whole crew arrived at the dunes.

"Jeff, what do you think will help protect these dunes?" asked Oliver.

"We could build a wooden fence or concrete wall," Jeff asserted. "But a fence might be hard to build sturdy enough in the sand."

"That's right. So instead, we are going to rope off the dunes to prevent drivers from parking on them and pedestrians from walking on them. We will just need to bury the wooden posts deep into the ground. Then we'll support them with rocks, clay, and sand and run a thick rope through all of them."

"It would also help if we grew some dune grass and sea oats," added Adam. "Those plants will protect and support the dunes with their strong roots."

"Great idea, Adam. That will help to maintain the dunes and increase the numbers of sea oats, an important native plant."

"We can also make some signs telling the drivers to stay away."

"I'll make them! I know what kind of signs will work," Scotty said with a large grin.

The whole crew worked for a couple of hours. By the end, they had strong wooden posts with a thick rope strung around them that prevented cars from parking on the dunes. There were also several creative signs in the ground to make sure the message was clear.

"I can't believe it is almost dusk," Oliver said, wiping some sand off of his jeans. "Thank you all so much for your generosity, hard work, and determination. Your contributions today have immensely improved our local environment. It is important to be proactive and practice the lessons we have learned every single day. This will help to prevent environmental emergencies in the future." Everyone smiled at each other, happy to have helped make a difference.

Oliver continued, "But there is one more project to do for now. I have asked an old, little, magical, gold-loving friend to assist me. Please meet me back at the nature center on June twenty-ninth," Oliver requested. "I am thinking of making this an annual tradition. Volunteers can meet up every year on Earth Day and help to clean and protect the environment."

The whole gang—Andrew, Scotty, Alvaro, Jeff, Adam, Rayana, and Eddie—gave one another congratulatory high fives and hugs. They were covered in dirt, sand, sweat, and mud, but they had smiles on their faces and joy in their hearts. They were proud of the hard work they had done to help protect and preserve the environment.

3

A Fresh Start

On June 29, everyone reconvened at the nature center greenhouse. They were surprised to find that it was all fixed up. It had shiny new windows and beds full of dark, rich composted soil, as well as beautiful flowers, vegetables, and fruits growing in great abundance.

"Oliver," Andrew said, "did you do all of this work by yourself?"

"Umm…let's just say I had a 'little' help from a 'little' friend."

This statement only confused everyone.

"I think you have been working too hard," asserted Scotty. "Next thing you know, you will be seeing leprechauns in the bushes!"

Oliver glanced over toward the bushes and whispered, "Thanks, Jake. I'll get you the rest of that gold later." Then he began the tour of the new and improved greenhouse. There was a vast amount of fresh herbs like mint, basil, parsley, sage, rosemary, and thyme, along with vines plentiful with heirloom tomatoes. Trays contained young, blossoming zinnias, geraniums, and gladiolas. There was even a bed teeming with a variety of young vegetables like zucchini, squash, carrots, and eggplants.

"You are an outstanding gardener, Oliver," said Eddie. "Where did you learn to garden like this?"

"I actually learned from my mother, Karen. But that's another story."

"This is a sight I could get used to," Lila said to Oscar, as they both watched over the humans toiling away in the garden. "I invited all of our animal friends to come enjoy this wonderful and momentous occasion with us."

Review and Critical Thinking Questions

1. What is runoff? What is a cause of runoff? What are some examples of things that make runoff worse? How can we help fix the runoff problem? How can we use the water saved by rain barrels?

2. Name some ways that having a local garden helps people and the environment. How can you help start a local garden? How does growing your own garden help reduce pollution?

3. What is composting? Why is it important? What are some benefits from using composted soil?

4. Explain the concept of reduce, reuse, and recycle. What is one way you can personally reduce the amount of waste you create? What is something that you personally reuse? What is a product that you or your family buy regularly that you can recycle? What is a product that you or your family buy regularly that cannot be recycled? Why is it bad to use "disposable" products?

5. Why are sand dunes and estuaries important? What can sand dunes help protect against? (Hint: It is the wearing away of sand and other land by wind, water, and other natural forces?) What is a common nickname for estuaries, since they are the place many animals come to reproduce near the sea?

6. Name a type of herb Oliver grows in the greenhouse. Name a type of flower Oliver grows in the greenhouse. Name a type of vegetable that Oliver grows in the greenhouse.

7. Why is it important to have strong communities? What are some ways having a strong community can help the environment? What is an organization that you can volunteer for in your own community?

I Spy Leprechauns

How many illustrations in this book feature Jake the Leprechaun? If you think it is just one, go back and take another look. How many illustrations can you find him in now?

Word search

Find these words in the puzzle below:

bacteria
community
conserve
disposable
erosion
flora
habitat
oliver
pond
reduce
tradition

biodegradable
compost
contaminate
ecology
estuary
generosity
lila
oscar
preserve
reuse
volunteer

brook
concern
decompose
environment
fauna
greenhouse
ocean
pest
recycle
river
weed

```
r e d u c e o s c a r n z w z
p r e s e r v e s t u a r y a
r e c y c l e n w d k e c r v
o u o o e t r a d i t i o n r
c o m m u n i t y a n l n w b
o l p j s e v d n o f a s c a
m i o w s a e i i r e f e o c
p v s u t e m s r c i k r n t
o e e p w a o p o o o v v c e
s r i o t r v o l u n t e e r
t g e n e r o s i t y m p r i
b i o d e g r a d a b l e n a
e c o l o g y b r o o k s n w
f a u n a d t l h a b i t a t
l i l a g r e e n h o u s e i
```

Jumble Time

Each set of jumble letters can be rearranged to make a word. Use the hints to help you solve the word jumble.

tesp   hint: something that can harm your garden and crops

urto   hint: guided trip

dwee   hint: An invasive, harmful plant

nopd   hint: small body of water

tsva   hint: large in size

rrvie   hint: body of water, usually flows into an ocean

naufa   hint: animals specific to an area

ceano   hint: large body of water

laitv   hint: extremely important or necessary

bushr   hint: small, tree-like plant

cureed   hint: make smaller in amount

ervpseer   hint: to maintain or keep something the same

durtsy   hint: strong or well built

ienturo   hint: regular actions or practices

lpthorae   hint: large or excessive in amount

eloocyg   hint: species found in the same habitat

cabtreai   hint: unicellular organisms

sidplbaeos   hint: something that is only used once

zeanlya   hint: study or examine thoroughly

itlasseen   hint: absolutely necessary; important

oueervltn   hint: free worker/laborer

ttraiondi   hint: a custom or regular practice

usoylgrovi   hint: to do with force and strength

plorovedveede   hint: having too many buildings and structures in one place

lbeaoibedrgead   hint: able to be broken down quickly by natural processes

Crossword Puzzle

Down:

1. A destructive insect or other animal that attacks crops, food, and livestock.

2. A building where plants can grow and be protected from harsh weather, animals, and other dangers.

3. The plants of a particular region, habitat, or geological period.

6. The natural home or environment of an animal, plant, or other organism. A particular type of environment regarded as a home for organisms.

9. He saves the nature center.

11. To turn materials like plastic and aluminum into new products instead of putting them in the trash, where they could take millions of years to decompose.

12. The animals of a particular region, habitat, or geological period.

15. The wise, old painted turtle from the story.

19. The first visible light of the sun in the morning.

Across:

4. To stop something from happening or arising.

5. Something important or essential.

7. Gradually take in or soak up a liquid or energy.

8. Concentrate on one thing and ignore distractions.

10. To deal with something before it becomes a problem.

13. The humorous and fun pug from the story.

14. A small stream, usually of fresh or brackish water.

16. A very large expanse of sea; in particular, each of the main areas into which the sea is divided geographically.

17. Make fun of or treat with ridicule.

18. Having rough, sharp, protruding points.

20. A small body of still water formed naturally or by hollowing or embanking.

(see answers in back of book to check your work!)

Wordmaster analogies

Choose the answer that best completes the analogy. What part of speech is each word? Is it a noun, adjective, verb, or adverb? Check for synonyms and antonyms. A synonym is word having the same or nearly the same meaning as another word. An antonym is a word opposite in meaning to another word. If you know these things about the words, it may help you find the correct answer.

Example:
banana : yellow ; strawberry : _____

A. fruit
B. vegetable
C. pineapple
D. red

1. biodegradable : banana peel ; disposable : _____

A. strawberry
B. towel
C. tomato
D. paper towel

2. zinnia : flora ; turtle : _____

A. reptile
B. sunflower
C. fauna
D. mammal

3. shrub : tree ; brook : _____

A. river
B. ocean
C. pond
D. brush

4. farms : agricultural pollution ; overdevelopment : _____

A. drainage
B. bacteria
C. runoff and flooding
D. rain barrel

5. essential : vital ; vast : _____

A. considerable
B. teeming
C. estuary
D. vigorously

6. school : teacher ; nature center : _____

A. volunteer
B. maintenance man
C. environmental educator
D. director

7. zinnias : flower ; eggplant : _____

A. fruit
B. gladiola
C. squash
D. vegetable

8. fragile : sturdy ; disposable : _____

A. reduce
B. reusable
C. cloth bag
D. bacteria

9. plethora : abundance ; considerable : _____

A. biodegradable
B. plentiful
C. abrasion
D. teeming

10. reusable : cloth bag ; recyclable : _____

A. toilet paper
B. paper towels
C. aluminum cans
D. styrofoam cups

Glossary

A

absorb *(verb)*: Gradually take in or soak up a liquid or energy.

abundance *(noun)*: A very large quantity of something.

agricultural pollution *(noun)*: The byproducts of farming practices that result in the contamination of the environment and surrounding ecosystems, and/or cause injury to humans and their economic interests.

analyze *(verb)*: Study or examine something thoroughly.

annual *(adjective)*: Occurring once per calendar year.

asserted *(verb)*: Confidently state a fact or belief.

attentively *(adverb)*: Paying very close attention to something.

awe *(noun)*: A feeling of great respect mixed with wonder.

awkwardly *(adverb)*: Uncomfortably or embarrassingly; without grace.

B

bacteria *(noun) (plural form of bacterium)*: A member of a large group of unicellular microorganisms that have cell walls but lack organelles and an organized nucleus, including some that can cause disease. Bacteria are found in soil, water, and air and on or in the tissues of plants and animals. Bacteria play a vital role in global ecology, since the chemical changes they bring about include those involving organic decay and nitrogen fixation.

benefit *(noun)*: An advantage or profit gained from something.

biodegradable *(adjective)*: A material or substance that can be decomposed by bacteria or other natural agents.

blossoming *(adjective)*: The state of a plant flowering.

brook *(noun)*: A small stream, usually of fresh or brackish water.

brush *(noun)*: Undergrowth, small trees, and shrubs.

C

carbon monoxide *(noun)*: An odorless, colorless poisonous gas that is emitted from car engines.

community *(noun)*: All the people living in a particular area or town, especially in the context of social values and responsibilities; society.

compost *(noun)*: Decayed organic material used as a plant fertilizer, or in a mixture used as a growing medium.

composting *(verb)*: The act of creating compost by using decaying organic materials.

concept *(noun)*: An idea, plan, or intention.

concern *(noun)*: A feeling of anxiety or responsibility for something or someone.

congratulate *(verb)*: Give praise to someone for an achievement.

conserve *(verb)*: Prevent waste or overuse of an important substance or material.

considerable *(adjective)*: Large in size, quantity, or amount.

contaminate *(verb)*: The act of making something impure by exposure to or addition of a poisonous or polluting substance.

contribution *(noun)*: The part played by a person in helping something to advance.

cutlery *(noun)*: utensils used to eat including forks, spoons, and knives.

D

dawn *(noun)*: The first visible light of the sun in the morning.

decay *(verb)*: To be broken down slowly by natural processes.

decompose *(verb)*: Break down or decay. While organic materials can often be decomposed in a short period of time, some man-made materials can take millions of years.

descend *(verb)*: Move downward to a lower elevation.

dilapidated *(adjective)*: A building or object in a state of ruin or disrepair due to neglect or age.

dire *(adjective)*: Of an urgent or serious situation or event.

disbelief *(noun)*: Inability to accept that something is real or true.

disposable *(adjective)*: Intended to be used once and then thrown away.

drought *(noun)*: A shortage of water from a long period without rain.

dumping grounds *(noun)*: A place where garbage or unwanted material is left. Some people dump materials rather than take the time to properly sort and recycle them.

dusk *(noun)*: The end of the day when the last rays of the sun are barely visible.

dwindling *(adjective)*: Diminishing gradually in size or strength.

E

ecology:

    1. *(noun)* A subdivision of biology that studies animals and other organisms and their environments.

    2. *(noun)* A set of species found in the same habitat or ecosystem at the same time.

ecosystem *(noun)*: A biological community of interacting organisms and their physical environment.

environment *(noun)*: The natural world as a whole or in a particular geographical area, especially as affected by human activity.

environmental educator *(noun)*: A person who teaches about how the planet's physical and biological systems work.

erosion *(noun)*: The process by which the surface of the Earth is worn away by wind, water, and other natural or man-made agents.

essential *(adjective)*: Absolutely necessary or important.

estuary *(noun)*: A body of water formed where freshwater from a river or stream flows into the ocean, mixing with seawater.

exhaust:

1. *(verb)* Use up (resources or reserves) completely. For example, "The country has exhausted its oil reserves."

2. *(noun)* Waste gases or air expelled from an engine, turbine, or other machine in the course of its operation. Exhaust from cars contains several compounds that are harmful to the environment.

F

fauna *(noun)*: The animals of a particular region, habitat, or geological period.

fertilizer *(noun)*: A chemical or natural substance added to soil or land to increase its ability to grow strong, healthy plants.

flora *(noun)*: The plants of a particular region, habitat, or geological period.

focus *(verb)*: Concentrate on one thing and ignore distractions.

fragile *(adjective)*: Easily damaged or broken.

G

generosity *(noun)*: The quality of being kind and sharing with or giving to others.

geranium *(noun)*: An herbaceous flowering plant that bears fruit that resembles the long bill of a crane.

greenhouse *(noun)*: A building where plants can grow and be protected from harsh weather, animals, and other dangers.

H

habitat *(noun)*: The natural home or environment of an animal, plant, or other organism. A particular type of environment regarded as a home for organisms.

I

immensely *(adverb)*: Extremely or to a great extent.

inconsiderate *(adjective)*: Ignoring the wants and needs of others.

interstate *(noun)*: Part of a system of express highways that cover the forty-eight contiguous United States.

J

jagged *(adjective)*: Having rough, sharp, protruding points.

K

kneel *(verb)*: To be in a position where the body is supported by the knees.

L

leprechaun *(noun)*: A small, mischievous being from Irish folklore.

M

manchego *(noun)*: A traditional Spanish cheese made from sheep's milk.

mock *(verb)*: Make fun of or treat with ridicule.

momentous *(adjective)*: An event or change that is of great importance, especially in regard to the future.

N

native plant *(noun)*: An indigenous plant that has developed or grown in the same area for many years. Native plants are usually well adapted to the specific geographical area where they live.

nature center *(noun)*: A nonprofit organization that promotes learning about the natural world, including ecology, biology, and environmentalism. Nature centers use many hands-on activities to increase curiosity in nature and wildlife. They also help to educate visitors on important environmental issues.

nourish *(verb)*: To give food, water, or other substances necessary for growth and good health.

O

ocean *(noun)*: A very large expanse of sea; in particular, each of the main areas into which the sea is divided geographically.

organic waste *(noun)*: A type of waste, typically originating from plant or animal material, that can be broken down in a short period of time by other living organisms.

overdeveloped *(adjective)*: A space or area that has an excessive amount of buildings and structures. Flooding and runoff can be a major problem in these areas.

overpackaged *(adjective)*: Products that are wrapped in more materials than are needed or desirable.

P

painted turtle *(noun)*: A species of reptile that has a brightly marked shell. These are the most widely distributed turtle in North America.

peninsula *(noun)*: A piece of land that is mostly surrounded by water but is still connected to the mainland.

pest *(noun)*: A destructive insect or other animal that attacks crops, food, and livestock.

pesticide *(noun)*: A substance used for destroying insects or other organisms harmful to cultivated plants or animals.

plentiful *(adjective)*: Yielding great or large quantities.

plethora *(noun)*: A large or excessive amount of something.

pollutants *(noun)*: A polluting substance, especially in regard to water or the atmosphere.

pollution *(noun)*: The presence in or introduction into the environment of a substance or thing that has harmful or poisonous effects.

pond *(noun)*: A small body of still water formed naturally or by hollowing or embanking.

portions *(noun)*: An amount, piece, or section of something.

preservative *(noun)*: A substance used to preserve foodstuffs or other materials against decay. Some preservatives can be harmful to humans if ingested.

preserve:

1. *(verb)* To maintain something in its original state; to keep safe from harm or injury.

2. *(noun)* An area where wildlife is protected.

prevent *(verb)*: To stop something from happening or arising.

proactive *(adjective)*: To deal with something before it becomes a problem.

R

rain barrel *(noun)*: A system that collects and stores rainwater that otherwise would be lost to runoff.

raw materials *(noun)*: The basic material from which a product is made. Many raw materials are finite and can be used up if not protected or recycled.

reconvened *(verb)*: To convene or meet up again, especially after a pause or break.

reduce, reuse, and recycle (verb): Three ways to reduce the amount of waste introduced into the environment. **Reduce** means to produce less waste by avoiding overpackaged products. **Reuse** means to use products like cloth bags and glass jars instead of disposable ones. **Recycle** means to turn materials like plastic and aluminum into new products instead of putting them in the trash, where they could take millions of years to decompose.

retain *(verb)*: Continue to hold on to or to keep something

river *(noun)*: A large natural stream of water flowing in a channel to the sea, a lake, or another such stream.

routine *(noun)*: Actions or practices done regularly.

runoff *(noun)*: The draining away of water (or substances carried in it) from the surface of an area of land into streams.

S

salt marsh *(noun)*: A piece of grassland that is regularly flooded by saltwater.

sand dunes *(noun)*: Ridges of sand created by the wind and waves. They act as a reservoir of sand after major storm systems.

self-defense *(noun)*: The defense, or guarding, of oneself, usually through physical means.

shrub *(noun)*: A woody plant that is smaller than a tree and has several main stems arising at or near the ground.

species *(noun)*: A group of organisms that can successfully breed—that is, that can exchange genes while creating offspring.

sternly *(adverb)*: To do with a serious, unrelenting manner, especially in an act of authority or discipline.

storm water *(noun)*: Surface water in an abnormal quantity resulting from heavy falls of rain or snow.

sturdy *(adjective)*: Solidly or strongly built.

T

teeming *(verb)*: To be full of or rich in amount.

toiling *(verb)*: Working extremely hard.

tour *(noun)*: A trip through a place in order to view or inspect it.

tradition *(noun)*: A custom or regular practice.

V

variety *(noun)*: A number of distinct things that are of the same general class or quality.

vast *(adjective)*: Immense or great in quantity or size.

vegetation *(noun)*: Plants considered collectively, especially those found in a particular area or habitat.

vigorously *(adverb)*: Forcefully, energetically and strongly.

vital *(adjective)*: Something important or essential.

volunteer *(noun)*: A person who freely offers to take part in a task without being paid. Volunteer workers are very important to nonprofit organizations, like nature centers, that operate on small budgets.

W

weed *(noun)*: A wild plant growing where it is not wanted and in competition with cultivated plants.

Z

zest *(noun)*: Rich with energy and enthusiasm.

zinnia *(noun)*: A widely cultivated American flower known for its bright colors.

Crossward answers

CPSIA information can be obtained
at www.ICGtesting.com
Printed in the USA
LVOW05*1344110216

472783LV00003BB/3/P